Dear Parent:
Your child's love

Every child learns to read in a different ~~~~~~~~~~~~~ speed. You can help your young reader improve and become more co..dent by encouraging his or her own interests and abilities. You can also guide your child's spiritual development by reading stories with biblical values and Bible stories, like I Can Read! books published by Zonderkidz. From books your child reads with you to the first books he or she reads alone, there are I Can Read! books for every stage of reading:

SHARED READING
Basic language, word repetition, and whimsical illustrations, ideal for sharing with your emergent reader.

1 BEGINNING READING
Short sentences, familiar words, and simple concepts for children eager to read on their own.

2 READING WITH HELP
Engaging stories, longer sentences, and language play for developing readers.

3 READING ALONE
Complex plots, challenging vocabulary, and high-interest topics for the independent reader.

4 ADVANCED READING
Short paragraphs, chapters, and exciting themes for the perfect bridge to chapter books.

I Can Read! books have introduced children to the joy of reading since 1957. Featuring award-winning authors and illustrators and a fabulous cast of beloved characters, I Can Read! books set the standard for beginning readers.

A lifetime of discovery begins with the magical words **"I Can Read!"**

Visit www.icanread.com for information on enriching your child's reading experience.
Visit www.zonderkidz.com for more Zonderkidz I Can Read! titles.

"Let wise people listen and add to what
they have learned."
Proverbs 1:5

ZONDERKIDZ

Listen Up, Larry
©2012 Big Idea Entertainment, LLC. VEGGIETALES®, character names, likenesses
and other indicia are trademarks of and copyrighted by Big Idea Entertainment, LLC.
All rights reserved.
Illustrations ©2011 by Big Idea Entertainment, Inc.

Requests for information should be addressed to:
Zonderkidz, 5300 *Patterson SE, Grand Rapids, Michigan* 49530

ISBN 978-0-310-73215-0

Editor: Mary Hassinger
Art direction: Karen Poth
Cover design: Karen Poth
Interior design: Ron Eddy

Printed in China

14 15 16 17 18 /DSC/ 6 5 4 3 2

ZONDERkidz

I Can Read!

BEGINNING 1 READING

Listen Up, Larry

story by Karen Poth

My name is Detective Larry.

This is my partner, Bob.

We solve mysteries.

Sometimes our jobs
are very messy.

Here is one of our stories.

Bob and I were out in the car.

RING!

A call came in.

There was a mess at Junior's house.

We drove there fast.

At the Asparagus house
Mom and Dad were
sitting at the table.
They looked sad.

They showed us Junior's
report card.
I looked at it very closely.

REPORT CARD

U	MATH
	CIENCE
	ELLING
	LISH
	CATION
	STUDIES

Junior had all U's.

That means "unsatisfactory."

That is not good.

I put the report card in a bag.

"We will figure this out,"

I told them.

"Larry," Bob whispered.
"You put the report card in
the bag with your lunch."
Oops!

Bob and I went to
Junior's school.
We hid in the closet.
We could see Junior.
I could also eat my lunch.

We found the problem.

Junior wasn't listening.

He was talking.

He was drawing.

"This is bad," Bob said.

"God wants us to listen.

That's how we learn."

"What did you say?"

I asked Bob.

I wasn't listening.

Bob had a plan.

"Meet me at Junior's house," he said.

I forgot how to get there.

Bob gave me directions.

But I wasn't listening.

My stuffed badger and I drove to Junior's.

We drove and drove.

"Junior's house is not this far,"

I told my badger.

We stopped at a gas station.

The peas there couldn't help us.

We were lost!

Really lost!

We got back in the car.

I wished I had listened to Bob!

We drove and drove and drove.

My badger was scared.

Finally, we found Junior's house.

We were very late.

The Asparagus family was in bed.

"Larry," Dad Asparagus said.

"Bob left a long time ago.

But we do have some good news."

"It is important to listen,"
Junior said from inside.

"Bob told us you were lost,"
Junior said, "because you didn't listen."

"I don't ever want to be
lost like that.
From now on, I am
going to listen!"

I thought about my
behavior.

I thought about Bob.

I wasn't very nice

to him.

I started to leave the house.

"Thanks," Junior said with a smile.

I went to get Bob.

We drove to a diner.

"I'm sorry I didn't listen to you,"

I told him on the way.

"Make a left here," Bob said.

I made a right.

I drove right up on

Mr. Nezzer's porch.

I wasn't listening again!

We got back on the road.

Bob gave directions to the diner.

This time I listened!